MY FUNNY FAMILY MOVES HOUSE

Chris Higgins
Illustrated by Lee Wildish

Hodder Children's Books

A division of Hachette Children's Books

For Baby Louis.
Another welcome addition to *my* funny
family which seems to be getting bigger
and bigger!
Thanks to Lauren.

Chapter 1

My mum is the luckiest person in the world.

She said so on her birthday last week. Her special thirtieth birthday. We made her Queen for the Day and put on a surprise Royal Variety Show for her in the church hall. Everybody came.

There were more than 200 people in the audience, mostly from our school. Even Mrs Dunnet (our headteacher), Mrs Shoutalot (my teacher), Miss Pocock (V's teacher), and Mr McGibbon (Stanley's teacher) plus his wife and kids came to watch. Everyone in our family was in the show except Mum, Dad and baby Will.

It was fun.

'I never knew I had such a talented family!' said Mum.

She's right, we are talented! But that's another story.

Now the Royal Variety Show is over, everything's gone a bit flat and boring. And crowded.

It's always crowded in our house. That's because there are nine of us in our family: Mum, Dad, my big brother Dontie, me, my sister V, my little brother Stanley, my little sister Anika, my baby brother Will, and Jellico the dog. Our ages range from thirty-two years to six weeks.

My name's Mattie and I'm nine.

Since Will arrived on Christmas Day our house feels like it's bursting at the seams. Will takes up a lot of room for a little baby.

Actually, it's not him, it's his stuff. We can't see the telly because his pram's in the way. And now V, Anika and I are packed like sardines into one bedroom, Mum, Dad and Will are squashed like tomatoes in another, and Dontie and Stanley are squeezed like toothpaste onto a single bed in the tiny third bedroom.

V says, 'This house is stunting my growth.'

Dontie says, 'This house is stunting my intellectual development.' This is because he wants his own computer in his room but Mum says 'No, and anyway, there's nowhere to put it.'

Grandma says, 'There's no room to swing a cat in here,' which is something she says quite a lot.

Mum says, 'It's a tight squeeze'.

Uncle Vez says, 'Stop moaning, the lot of you. When I was a youngster we slept ten to a bed and it didn't do us any harm.' But I think he's fibbing.

Uncle Vez is Mum's foster father. He's very old and looks like a garden gnome.

Grandma and Granddad are Dad's mum and dad. They're nearly as old as Uncle Vez.

Uncle Vez and Grandma and Granddad spend a lot of time in our house. Today the only one who's missing is Dad, and he's not far away. He's out in the shed, painting a picture.

It's Saturday afternoon and Grandma's come over to help, but somehow she's making things worse. She's got the ironing board out and is tackling a jumble of school uniform with an angry, spitting iron. Anika and Jellico streak past, get tangled in the lead and pull it out of the socket. The iron topples over and Mum grabs it before it hits Stanley who is lying on the floor reading.

'Ouch! That's hot!' she says and slams down the iron. The pile of newly-pressed clothes topples onto the floor.

Mum's had enough.

'I know Grandma means well,' she hisses, holding her hand under the cold tap. She sounds like the fizzing iron. 'But she just gets in the way. Hasn't she got a home to go to?'

I've noticed Mum gets a bit short-tempered when she's feeling crowded. And our house is fit to bursting at the moment because it's the middle of winter and the weather's bad and we can't go out to play.

It's not Grandma's fault. We're all the same. We keep tripping over each other and stepping on Jellico and sitting on baby Will and breaking things every time we turn around.

The kitchen is hot and steamy and there's washing hanging everywhere. Last night I came downstairs for a drink in the middle of the night and screamed with fright, waking everyone up. Wet babygros were dangling from cupboards and worktops like scary baby ghosts.

'What I'd give for a tumble dryer!' moans Mum.

'We could get you one,' offers Grandma, who's feeling really bad about Mum's hand.

'No thanks!' says Mum, automatically. 'We can manage.' Then she adds with a sigh, 'There's no room for one anyway.'

She's right, you know. You couldn't cram another thing into our house if you tried.

Chapter 2

In school we're doing division.

My sister V is brilliant at numeracy. I'm not. I don't really get the point of it. It's not my teacher's fault – Mrs Shoutalot is very enthusiastic and tries to make it *interesting* and *relevant*.

'How many people live in your house?' she shouts at us.

A forest of hands shoot up.

'Alfie?'

'Three, Miss.'

'How many rooms do you have in your house, Alfie?'

Alfie counts them on his fingers. 'The living room – one, the kitchen – two, Mum's bedroom – three, my bedroom – four, my sister's bedroom – five, the bathroom – six.'

'Six rooms. Excellent. So how many rooms is that for each person living in your house?'

Alfie looks as blank as I do, while all around us hands wave excitedly in the air.

'Divide the number of rooms by the number of people,' explains Mrs Shoutalot. 'Divide six by three and what do you get?'

'Two, Miss?'

'Brilliant!' booms our teacher. 'In

Alfie's house there are two rooms per person. Who wants to try next? Tia?'

Wow! Two whole rooms for each person. And I haven't even got a bedroom to myself.

Tia's got 2.5 rooms for each person in her house. That's two and half rooms each!

'I know! Let's make a graph on the whiteboard for the whole class!' shouts Mrs Shoutalot, who has lots of good ideas. 'Work out how many rooms there are in your house per person, and as soon as you've got the answer put your hand up. Morgan? You're fast!'

Morgan's got four people and eight rooms in his house. That means he's got two rooms for each person in his family as well. Easy-peasy. Mrs Shoutalot writes his name on the graph next to Alfie's. Beside me Lucinda is scribbling away like mad.

'Holly?'

'Um … Five people, nine rooms, 1.6 rooms per person,' says Holly (who's brainy at maths). She gets it right, and her name goes on the graph beneath Morgan's.

'Lucinda?'

'I haven't worked it out yet, Miss,' says Lucinda, still scribbling.

'Lewis?'

Lewis has got 1.8. Mrs Shoutalot inserts his name between Morgan's and Holly's.

Kayleigh, who lives in a flat, has got 1.25. That's one and a quarter rooms each. Her name is written beneath Holly's.

I get this! Bending my head over my maths book I work it out carefully. Three bedrooms, one kitchen, one living room, one bathroom. Six divided by nine. Better check.

'Miss? Do I count Jellico?'

'Who's Jellico?'

'Our dog.'

'No, Mattie. No pets, just people.'

Divided by eight.

'Miss? Do I count Uncle Vesuvius?'

Mrs Shoutalot clears her throat. 'Oh dear. This is getting more complicated than I thought. Does he live with you, Mattie?'

'No.'

'No then. Lucinda? Are you ready now?'

'Yes, Miss.' Lucinda puts down her pencil and reads aloud from the notes she's been making. 'There are three people in my house, Mum, Dad and me. Upstairs we've got five bedrooms, all ensuite, so that's ten rooms in fact, plus a dressing-room, family bathroom and Dad's study. Downstairs, we've got a living room, sitting room, dining room, breakfast room, den, kitchen, utility room, cloakroom, wet room and conservatory.'

The class stares at her in stunned silence.

'Oops!' says Lucinda. 'I forgot! We've a granny annexe in the garden but we haven't got a granny in it. Does it count?'

'No,' says Mrs Shoutalot faintly. This is very unusual for her because normally she shouts. 'Definitely not.'

'Thought not,' says Lucinda. 'So that means we've got twenty-three rooms between three people. That's 7.66 to the second decimal point.'

That was good working out. But my teacher doesn't say 'Well done!' She just puts Lucinda's name at the top of the chart and writes 7.66 beside it. Then she says, 'Right, I think that will do for now,' and puts down her pen.

'Aw, Miss! Mattie hasn't had her turn yet,' says Lucinda.

'Nor me!'

'Nor me!'

Everyone is clamouring for their go. It's been a fun lesson.

'Maybe this wasn't such a good idea after all,' says Mrs Shoutalot under her breath. I don't think she means anyone to hear her, but I do.

'*Pleeeeease* Miss!'

'I've worked it out!'

'*I* want a go!'

In the end we all get a turn. It's only fair.

In our house we have eight people, not including Jellico, and six rooms. My answer is 0.75.

'Well done Mattie, you've worked it out beautifully,' says Mrs Shoutalot and writes my name and 0.75 at the very bottom of the chart.

I smile happily. That was a good lesson. I understand division now. And I've learned something else as well.

Now I know that in our house we have less than one room each and in Lucinda's they have more than seven each.

No wonder it's a tight squeeze in our house.

Chapter 3

'Lucinda's got ten times more space in her house than we've got in ours,' I tell Mum on the way home.

'Lucky old Lucinda,' says Mum. Then she adds, 'How do you know?'

'We did it in numeracy.'

'Really?' She looks surprised.

'She's got twenty-three rooms.'

'Twenty-three!' Mum says longingly, and I wish I hadn't told her now.

WORRY ALERT!

But then she says, 'I'm glad *I* don't have twenty-three rooms to clean!' in her normal voice and it's all right again.

We stop at Kumar's to buy our tea. Mum ties Jellico to the newspaper stand.

'Egg, beans and chips,' says Mum before we go in. 'So don't ask for anything else.'

'Can't we have sausages?' says V automatically and Mum snaps, 'What did I say?'

WORRY ALERT!

Money's tight. Again.

In case you haven't noticed, I'm a bit of worrier.

Inside the shop Mum places a dozen eggs, two tins of beans and a bag of frozen chips on Will's pram and waits to be served. Anika picks up till receipts from the floor and puts them in her pocket. She says they're treasure. When she's finished doing that she starts stroking a packet of crumpets. She loves crumpets. Stanley stands at the freezer staring at the cheesecakes and tubs of ice-cream. Mum ignores them both. V is sulking because she's been told off, but Mum ignores her too.

The lady in front of us has a big trolleyful of food. While Mr Kumar is ringing through her shopping she keeps adding things to it.

She picks up a packet of chocolate ginger biscuits (yum!) and then reaches for the crumpets Anika is stroking. 'May I?' she says and Anika hands them to her with a smile. The lady smiles back and drops them into her trolley.

V and Stanika (that's what we call Stan and Anika when they're together) watch longingly as pizza, cake and piles of other yummy stuff disappear from the lady's trolley into her shopping bags.

'Can we have pizz …?'

'No!' says Mum, and V's mouth clamps shut.

'Is that lady rich?' asks Stanley in a loud whisper.

Mum and the lady laugh but their faces go pink like they're both embarrassed. I don't think you're meant to ask if people are rich. Or poor. Not in front of them, anyway.

'Somebody's rich,' says Mr Kumar as he gives the lady her change. 'I just heard on the radio someone round here won one and a half million on the lottery last Saturday.'

'One and a half million,' says Mum faintly.

'Who is it?' asks the lady.

'They don't know. The ticket hasn't been claimed. It's not you, is it?'

The lady laughs. 'No chance. I don't play.'

'Me neither,' says Mum. But she sounds like she wished that she did.

'That's me done.' The lady tucks her change into her purse and snaps it shut. Then she takes the packet of crumpets from the top of her bag and gives it to Anika. 'There you are, sweetheart. That's for being a good girl.'

Anika's eyes shine with joy. But Mum whips them straight out of her hands and plonks them back in the lady's.

'No thank you.'

'Mu-um?' protests V, as Anika opens her mouth to wail.

'I said NO!' says Mum, raising her voice and Anika howls. The lady goes *bright* red this time, stuffs the crumpets back into her bag and leaves.

I want to die.

That rich, kind lady will think my mum is really rude and she's not. Normally.

Mum pays for her stuff without another word and marches out of the shop. She doesn't wait for us but charges up the street with the pram, Jellico lolloping along beside her, his leg caught in the lead. I grab Anika by the hand and she grabs Stanley and he grabs V and we all chase after her.

'Mum?' I say, catching up with her at last. 'Why …?' And then I stop.

MASSIVE ENORMOUS WORRY ALERT!

Mum dashes tears away with the back of her hand but it's too late, I've seen them.

'We're not a charity case, Mattie,' she sniffs, then she bends down and hugs us all tight to her.

'Now don't you go worrying that head of yours, Mattie Butterfield!' she scolds, because she knows what I'm like. 'We're fine. Everything's all right.'

But it's not. She's fibbing. I know she is.

Chapter 4

My dad's home! It's a half day at the college where he teaches art. He's making stew for tea – we're not having eggs, beans and chips after all! I love my dad's stew.

Mum disappears into the living room with him and baby Will while the rest of us do our homework at the kitchen table. I've got more division to do. It's easy now it makes sense.

Stanley and V have got reading.

V couldn't read for ages, then Grandma worked out that she couldn't see the words properly. Now she's got glasses she reads really well. Stan's brilliant at reading and won a prize at school. Anika hasn't got any homework because she's not old enough to go to school yet, but she pretends she has and draws nice round smiley faces with legs coming out of them which are meant to be us. My head's got a blob on it (my hat).

It's nice in our kitchen with Jellico

licking our feet and knees under the table, and delicious stew smells wafting around.

I look up. Mum is standing in the doorway with her arms folded, watching us. Dad's got one arm round her and a sleeping Will in the other. She's got a calm face now. I remember her crying face and say, 'Stew's better than crumpets.'

I'm not sure this is true, but it makes Mum and Dad laugh anyway. So I add for good measure, 'I'm glad our house hasn't got twenty-three rooms. It's perfect as it is.'

Mum shakes her head and sighs. 'It's not, Mattie. A few more rooms wouldn't come amiss. But it'll do.'

'It'll have to,' says Dad and plants a kiss on her head.

But I *do* think it's perfect. At this moment anyway.

Maybe not an hour later, when Anika's crying in the bath because she's got soap in her eyes and she doesn't want Mum, she wants Stanley. But Stanley has to sit at the kitchen table till he's finished all his stew.

And in the living room, Dontie's in trouble with Dad for not wanting his tea because he ate a burger on the way home from school, and Dad tells him to stop wasting money but Dontie says, 'It's *my* money, not yours, and anyway, I'll have my stew later,' and Dad says 'No, you won't!' and **TEMPERS ARE RISING!**

V yells, 'Stop arguing! I'm trying to watch the telly!' but Dad says, 'It's too late for television,' switches it off, and sends her to bed.

Will is screaming his head off because he needs a feed but Mum's tied up with Anika.

And I can't do my reading for school because V's shouting 'IT'S NOT FAIR!' in our bedroom and punching the pillows, and Dontie and Dad are arguing in the living room, and Will's bawling for his feed in Mum and Dad's bedroom, and Anika's screeching in the bathroom, and Stanley's got to sit in the kitchen on his own till he's eaten all his stew and then go *straight* to bed for being naughty.

Maybe it would be nice to have a bigger house after all. Like Mum said, a few more rooms wouldn't come amiss. Or even one teeny-weeny room. A peace and quiet room, where I could get my reading done, so I wouldn't get shouted at by Mrs Shoutalot the next day.

But it's not going to happen, is it?

I might as well wish that we could go to London to see the Queen, or sail around the world, or fly to the moon for our summer holidays as buy a bigger house. You need lots of money to do things like that.

And we don't have lots of money. We don't have much money at all.

It's a tight squeeze in our house in more ways than one.

Chapter 5

A bit later on, I'm the only one snuggled up on the sofa between Mum and Dad.

Will's fast asleep in his cot now he's had a feed.

In our bedroom Anika is snoring gently. In the bed next to her, V is still sulking.

Stanley's supposed to be asleep, but we all know he's reading under the covers by torchlight.

Dontie's eating his stew in the kitchen now he's hungry.

Snuggling up on the sofa between Mum and Dad is known as having a cuddle sandwich in our house. It's the best kind of sandwich there is.

'Fancy some toast?' asks Dad.

'Yes please!' Actually, hot, buttery toast is pretty good too. In a different way.

'Make sure there's enough bread left for the morning,' says Mum automatically.

Dad makes Mum a steaming mug of tea as well.

'Better now?' he asks.

'Yes,' she says, licking the butter off her fingers. Sometimes my mum looks like a teenager. The bell rings and she groans.

'*Please*,' she says, 'tell me that's not your mother?'

I run to open the front door.

'It *is* Grandma, Mum. And Granddad.'

Grandma looks surprised. 'Were you expecting us?'

'Sort of.'

Mum switches on her smile and says, 'Cup of tea?'

'No, we're not stopping,' says Grandma. 'We just thought we'd call in on the way past because ...' And then she breaks off.

'Because what?' asks Dad, but Grandma just stands there looking bashful like Anika when she doesn't know what to say next.

'She's got this thing in her head ...' starts Granddad, and Mum says, 'What have I done now?'

She's laughing but she sort of means it. Dad said once that Mum and Grandma have a *love/hate* relationship. That worried me a lot, not the *love* bit but the *hate*, till Mum explained it just meant that they rub each other up the wrong way occasionally. Well, quite a lot, actually.

'Nothing!' says Grandma. 'It's just that ...'

'Just what?' We stare at her in surprise. It's not like Grandma to be lost for words.

'Well, call me stupid,' she says, 'but have you heard that someone from round here has won a million and a half pounds on the lottery?'

'Oh, that?' says Mum, looking grumpy again. 'Yes.'

'Is it you?' asks Dontie excitedly, appearing from the kitchen.

'No,' says Grandma and I remember last Saturday night, on Mum's birthday,

Grandma checking her ticket and saying, 'Not me,' and crumpling it up.

'Is it someone else we know?' asks V, poking her head round the door.

'I'm not sure. No one's come forward yet,' says Grandma, looking a bit flustered. 'I just can't help wondering …' Her voice trails away.

'Wondering what?' asks Dad, bemused.

'Well, I know it sounds silly, but I wondered if it could be you?'

Chapter 6

Dad gawps at Grandma.

'Us? We don't do the lottery.'

'I know that,' says Grandma. 'Normally. But you had a ticket last Saturday.'

'Did we?' Dad looks baffled.

'Uncle Vez bought Mum one as a birthday present. It was in her card.' It's Stanley's turn to pop up. He's been earwigging on the stairs.

Mum sits bolt upright. 'Yes, he did,

you're right! I'd forgotten all about it.'

'Did you check it?' asks Granddad.

'No, I don't think I did. There was too much going on. Anyway, nobody round here wins the lottery, do they?'

'Somebody has,' says Granddad. 'Where's your ticket?'

'I haven't a clue,' says Mum.

'It'll still be in the card,' says Dontie, and grabs Uncle Vez's beautiful flowery card off the mantelpiece. But it's not there. He looks through all the cards one by one, giving them all a shake, but he can't find it. Then he looks behind the clock. It's not there either.

'Search the bin!' orders Grandma. Suddenly she's stopped being flustered and turned into Sherlock Holmes. We do as we're told, emptying it out on the floor. But it's just full of apple cores, dirty tissues and an old plaster, so she makes us put them all back again. Yuck!

Then we go through *all* the bins and *all* the recycling but it's nowhere to be found.

'Ohhhh!' says V. 'It's not fair. You lost the winning ticket, Mum.'

'No I didn't! We don't even know if it *was* the winning ticket, Vera-Lynn,' says Mum, giving V her full name, which shows she's getting cross. But I have a feeling that really it's herself she's cross with, not V.

'What were you wearing?' asks Grandma, sounding more and more like a real detective every minute. Mum's face lights up.

'The new top and jeans you bought me for my birthday. I bet it's in the back pocket!'

She charges upstairs two at a time while we wait at the bottom, V and I squeezing each other's hands for luck. But when she comes back down and flops onto the sofa looking fed up, we know she hasn't found it.

'Where were you sitting?' asks Grandma, who won't let up.

'Right here,' says Mum. 'But there's no point, we won't find it.'

'Yes we will,' says Grandma, 'if it kills me! Up you get.'

You don't mess with Grandma.

Mum stands up and Grandma whips the cushions off the sofa, not just the pretty ones but the ones you sit on as well.

Here is a list of surprising things that we find down the sides of our sofa.

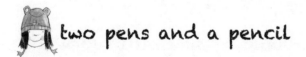 two pens and a pencil

V's hairclip, the one she lost ages ago

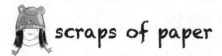 scraps of paper

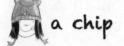 Stan's grey sock

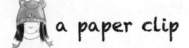 a chip

a paper clip

lots of soft crisps that don't taste nice (I tried one)

one of Anika's ribbons

a penny, a ten pence piece and a pound coin

a piece of spaghetti (cooked)

Christmas chocolate wrappers

biscuit crumbs

toast crumbs

 a fork

and … tucked down in the corner scrunched up in a ball …

 one lottery ticket.

Grandma pounces on it, smooths it out and presents it to Mum. 'Happy Birthday, Mona,' she says with a triumphant smile.

Chapter 7

'We still don't know if it's the winning ticket,' says Mum, but her eyes are shining and I know she thinks it is.

'How can we find out?' I ask.

'I'll check it on the computer,' says Dad, and we all crowd round to watch. But the Internet is down.

'Take it up to Kumar's, he's still open. He can put it through his machine,' says Granddad.

'No, I'm too scared!' says Mum.

'Give it to me,' says Dad.

'Wait for me, I'm coming with you!' says Granddad.

'And me!' says Grandma.

'Oh flip, we'll all go!' says Mum. 'This is a special occasion. Kids, get your coats on. Tim, you get Anika and I'll fetch Will.'

We're all going out in the cold and dark, even our new baby who was fast asleep in his cot!

'Where we going?' asks Anika sleepily when Dad carries her downstairs wrapped in a blanket.

'Hunting for treasure,' says Dad, and Anika, all her dreams come true, snuggles into him happily.

Mr Kumar looks surprised when we all troop into his shop.

'What's this? A family outing?'

'Have they found the lottery winner?' asks Dad.

'Not yet.'

'Give him the ticket, Tim,' says Granddad. 'We found this down the side of the chair. You never know, we might be lucky.'

Mr Kumar's eyes open very wide when Dad hands him the lottery ticket. We all watch in silence as he places it in the machine. I'm afraid to breathe.

Then Mr Kumar takes it out again and hands it back to Dad.

'I'm sorry, Mr Butterfield,' he says, looking sad. 'Better luck next time.'

Chapter 8

'Oh, Mona,' says Grandma, looking like she's going to cry. 'I'm sorry too. I shouldn't have raised your hopes like that. But I was so certain you had the winning ticket.'

'Never mind,' says Mum. 'Let's all go home and have a cup of tea.'

'Or something stronger,' says Dad.

'Good idea,' says Granddad, and buys drinks and crisps from Mr Kumar.

Back at home we have lemonade and

crisps for the kids, and something stronger for the grown-ups. It's like a party, only not much fun.

Anika, still inside the blanket, gives a huge yawn. 'Where's the treasure?'

'We didn't find any,' says Stan sadly.

Anika leans over and presses the corners of his mouth to make him smile. But even Stan doesn't feel like smiling. She frowns, then wriggles off Dad's knee and wanders upstairs, trailing her blanket behind her.

'Where's she off to?' says Grandma.

'Back to bed, I should think,' says Mum. 'She's tired out, bless her. I'd better get this little mite down too.' She stands up with Will in her arms. But Anika appears again, clutching some pieces of paper.

'What have you got?' asks Grandma.

'Treasure,' she says solemnly and gives

it to Stanley.

'It's till receipts from Kumar's,' explains Mum. 'And other stuff. She calls it her treasure and keeps it under her pillow. She's trying to cheer you up, Stan.'

'Aahhh!' says Grandma. 'Little sweetheart. Have you got any treasure to cheer Grandma up as well?'

Anika takes some of the receipts out of Stanley's hands and gives them to Grandma instead. Everybody laughs.

'See,' says Dad. 'It works.'

'Let's see what my treasure is,' says Grandma, making a game of it for Anika. She reads aloud,

'Spaghetti hoops
Sandwich loaf
Marmalade
Toothpaste

'Ooh!' she says to Anika. 'That is real treasure. Shall we see what the next one says?'

Anika giggles.

'Naan bread

Korma sauce

Poppadums

'Yummy! Someone's going to make a curry.'

'More!' orders Anika.

'Shall I read another one?'

'She'll be here all night,' says Mum, rolling her eyes. I think she means Grandma, not Anika.

'Last one,' says Grandma. But then she stops and stares at the piece of paper in her hand as if she can't believe her eyes.

'What's wrong?' asks Mum.

'Look everybody,' says Grandma.

'Look what Anika found.'

She holds up the piece of paper.

It's not a till receipt at all.

It's another lottery ticket.

Chapter 9

'Where did she get that from?' asks Mum in astonishment. 'She's a little magpie, that child. You can't leave anything lying around.'

Anika makes a dash for Stanley and buries her face in his lap. She thinks she's in trouble.

Grandma sits there thinking, her brain ticking and clicking like she's doing division. At last, her face clears.

'Anika? Did this treasure come out of

Mummy's birthday card, by any chance?'

'Floor!' says Anika, afraid to look up.

'You found it on the floor? Clever girl. Show Grandma where you found it.'

Anika raises her head. She's not in trouble after all. She gets down on her fat little tummy and points under the sofa.

'That's it! She's found the missing lottery ticket,' Grandma tells Mum. 'The one Uncle Vez bought you for your birthday!'

'Lucky for us Anika found this one and put it away safely,' says Dad, and everyone beams at my naughty little sister. Anika puts her hand out.

'Treasure?' she asks hopefully.

'Probably not,' laughs Mum. 'We still don't know if it's the winning ticket.' Which is what she said last time. But then she adds. 'I think I'll hang on to it though. Just in case.'

Anika's face falls. It lights up again when Dad says, 'I think we'd better go on another treasure hunt. Just in case.'

So we do. All of us. Grandma, Granddad, Mum, Dad, Dontie, V, Stanika, Will, Jellico and me. We all put on our coats (not Jellico) and troop back up to Kumar's.

'Found another ticket?' asks Mr Kumar

as we all file into the shop.

'Anika did,' says Mum and lets her give it to him.

This time his eyes don't open very wide. We watch closely as he puts the ticket in the machine. Then he takes it back out again and hands it back to Anika.

I let out a big sigh of disappointment. It's no good. We haven't won.

'Take good care of that, young lady,' he says. His voice sounds high and squeaky.

Mr Kumar coughs and clears his throat. In his normal voice he adds, 'You need to contact the lottery company by telephone as soon as possible.'

Chapter 10

WE WON! The lady from the lottery company came round the next day to confirm. She wanted us to go on television and tell everyone.

We were all very excited about being on TV.

'We'll be famous!' said Dontie.

'We'll be celebrities!' squealed V.

'We'll be in *Hello!* Or *OK!*' laughed Mum. These are posh magazines she reads when she's getting her hair done.

But Grandma shook her head. 'We'll think about it,' she said. After the lady had gone she said, 'Best not to tell anyone.'

'Why not?' asked Mum.

Grandma tapped the side of her nose with her finger which made her look very wise. 'You know. The green-eyed monster.'

Stanika stared at her, wide-eyed.

'What's the green-eyed monster?' asked V nervously.

'Jealousy,' said Grandma. 'Do you really want all that publicity?'

'She's got a point,' said Dad, looking *very* serious.

That night I couldn't sleep. I know that if someone is jealous of you, they say or do nasty things. V was jealous

of Stanley because he was a better reader than her, and she ripped up his prize book. It was the worst moment of my life, even worse than when Dontie fell off the cliff on holiday.

I didn't want anyone ripping up my books.

All night long I tossed and turned, worrying about *publicity* and *jealousy* and the *green-eyed monster*. In the end I sat up in bed and turned the light on.

Mum's head appeared round the door, all bleary-eyed and bed-haired. 'What are you doing, Mattie?'

'Making a Worry List. You told me to if I was worried.'

'I didn't mean at two o'clock in the morning. You'll wake the others up.'

This was not true at all. Next to me V and Anika were snoring loudly.

'All right,' sighed Mum and climbed wearily into bed beside me. 'Tell me what you're worried about.'

I read out what I'd written so far.

 Lucinda will tear up my books.

 Naughty George will pull my hair.

 Dennis will pinch my new hat and chuck it round the playground.

'What do you mean?' Mum looked

baffled. 'Lucinda's not going to tear your books up.'

'She might do. If she's got the green-eyed monster.'

'Oh, I *see*!' Mum put her arm round me and gave me a hug. Then she said, 'Maybe it might be a good idea to keep this to ourselves after all.'

The next day Mum and Dad told the lottery lady that we wanted no publicity. Then they sat us all down and told us not to tell anyone about our win.

We've never had a family secret before.

Chapter 11

On Saturday we all go on a **MAMMOTH** shopping expedition. We are allowed to choose whatever we want!

Here is a list of what people pick:

Will: a brand new pram, smaller than the old one, that will convert to a buggy when he's bigger. (Actually, Mum chooses this for him but he seems happy.)

Dontie: a Nintendo DS

Stanley: a bookcase to keep all his books in

V: a karaoke machine

Dad: some new paints

Anika: a pretty box to keep all her treasures in

Mum: a shiny mac
from Top Shop,
her favourite shop,
and a shiny bag
to go with it

We also buy a beautiful vase
for Grandma, a golf club for
Granddad (the kind you play
with, not the one you belong to)
and a wheelbarrow for Uncle Vez.
Everyone gets what they want.

Except me.

Will starts to get grizzly.

'Come on Mattie, make your
mind up!' says Dad.

But there's too much to
choose from.

'What about something for your bedroom?' asks Mum.

But there's no room in my bedroom for anything else. Especially now V's got a karaoke machine.

'Something for school?' suggests Dad.

But there's nothing I need.

'Something to play with?' says Dontie.

'Something pretty to wear?' says V.

'Something to read?' says Stanley.

It's all too much. I wish they'd stop going on at me. Suddenly I let out an enormous wail which makes everyone jump, including me.

'I don't know! I can't decide!'

'That's it!' says Mum crossly. 'We're going home right now. Will needs a feed.'

I've spoilt the day for everyone. We walk home in a line with Mum at the front, pushing my baby brother who's bawling his head off, Dad pushing the new pram, Dontie pushing the wheelbarrow with the presents in it, V, Stanley, Anika, and me, sobbing at the back.

All of a sudden, I stop dead. I've spotted something in the window of a house. It's a sign.

'Come on, Mattie!' shouts Dad. 'Stop dawdling.'

Mum turns the pram around to come and fetch me. 'What is it now?' she sighs.

'Look!'

Mum reads the sign.

'Oh no!' she says. 'Not a good idea.'

'But Mum ...'

'No, Mattie. I've got enough to look after!'

'*I'll* look after it ...'

Everyone walks back to see what we are looking at. The sign says:

BABY RABBITS FOR SALE

'I'll give her a hand,' says Dontie.

'You said we could choose whatever we wanted,' Stan points out.

'It's only fair,' says V.

'Stop ganging up on me!' protests Mum.

'Please Mum! Can we just see?'

'Go on then,' she says wearily. 'But we're not having one, I'm telling you now. I couldn't look after another thing. Not even a pot plant.'

There's only one left. He's soft and white and furry with pink eyes and a twitchy nose. I cradle him in my arms,

rubbing my face against his warm,
quivery body.

'I love him,' I say, and I really do.

'He's tickly,' says V.

'He's got the hiccups,' says Stan.

'He *is* beautiful,' says Mum, stroking
him. Her face has gone soft, like it does
when she looks at Will. Then Mum says,
'What shall we call him?' and I can't

believe my ears.

'Hiccup,' says Anika, and we all laugh because it's perfect.

'We need a hutch!' says V.

'Uncle Vez will knock one up for us,' says Dad.

We pop Will into the new pram and Hiccup into the old one, and wheel them both home with our shopping piled high in the wheelbarrow.

'My goodness,' says Mr Kumar who's standing in his shop doorway as we go past. 'Have you won the lottery?' He gives us a wink and goes back inside the shop.

He knows our secret, but no one else does and he's promised not to tell.

When we get home from shopping we phone Uncle Vez and Grandma and

Granddad and invite them over to give them their presents.

Granddad likes his golf club.

Grandma loves her vase.

Uncle Vez is over the moon with his new wheelbarrow.

'You shouldn't have spent all that money on me,' he says.

'You're the one who bought the ticket,' says Mum. 'It's your prize really.'

'No!' says Uncle Vez, looking alarmed. 'I told you, I don't want it. It was a present for you. What would I do with all that money?'

Mum gives Uncle Vez a big hug. Then she turns to Dad.

'What are *we* going to do with it? That's the point.'

Chapter 12

A man in a suit and a lady with a briefcase arrive from the lottery to help us decide what to do with the money. They have a long, long chat with Mum and Dad over tea and chocolate biscuits. We have to be really quiet so they can concentrate. There's nowhere to sit because they take up the entire sofa, so we stand next to them and listen.

'You'll never need to worry about money again,' says the lady.

'Did you hear that Mattie?' says Mum and I nod happily.

'Invest wisely and your money will do all the work for you,' says the man and in my head I see lots of pound coins with arms and legs digging our garden and cleaning our windows and putting our washing out on the line and it makes me giggle.

But then he starts talking about things like *shares* and *bonds* and *generating an income* and *self-invested personal pensions* and it gets really boring. Even Mum and Dad look a bit glassy-eyed.

After a while Anika starts stroking the lady's leg. At first the lady smiles but then I notice her pulling away a bit as if she wishes Anika would stop. But my little sister can't. She always strokes things she likes and she likes the lady's shiny tights.

V keeps helping herself to biscuits until Mum tells her off for being greedy. V explains that she's hungry because she's had to stand up for a long time being as the man and lady are taking up all the room on the sofa and talking so much.

'Don't be rude,' says Mum and makes her apologise. After that V stands there with her arms folded, looking grumpy.

Then Will wakes up and starts crying for his feed. Anika, still devotedly stroking the lady's shiny leg, accidentally knocks the cup of tea balanced on the lady's shiny knee into the man's lap.

The man jumps up with a shout and makes Jellico bark, then he wolfs down all the biscuits (Jellico, not the man) and she starts crying (Anika, not the lady)

and Mum is *mortified*.

When the man comes back from the bathroom he's wearing a pair of Dad's baggy old painting trousers. They look funny with his suit jacket and shirt and tie. But nobody laughs.

The man sits back down on the sofa and announces, 'I've been thinking.' So we all gather round to hear what he has to say. It's the least we can do.

'I think the very best use you could make of your money is to buy a house big enough for all of you to sit down in,' he says.

Mum and Dad smile at each other.

'That sounds like a good idea,' says Dad.

'That sounds like a *very* good idea,' agrees Mum.

So that's what we're going to do.

Chapter 13

In the middle of our kitchen table is a big pile of brochures. The pile is getting bigger by the day – soon we won't be able to see over it!

The brochures contain estate agents' details.

If you want to buy a house you ring up an estate agent (that's a person who sells houses) and he or she sends you a shiny brochure with pictures and interesting facts about houses for sale. Dad reads them out to us while we're eating our tea.

Dad: 'What do you think of this one? A superb, brand-new, detached, five bedroomed, family home ...'

Me: '*Five* bedrooms!'

Dad: '... with private, south-facing gardens, laid mainly to lawn, and a children's play area ...'

V: 'Let's buy that one!'

Dad: 'Ground floor: spacious kitchen/diner with built in oven, hob and hood ...'

Mum: 'Mmm. Nice!'

Me: 'What's a hob and hood?'

Dad: '... dual aspect sitting room opening out onto a sun deck...'

Stanley: 'What's dual aspect?'

V: 'What's a sun deck?'

Dad: '... plus family bathroom. First floor: master bedroom with en-suite bathroom and outstanding views.'

Mum: 'Wow! I like this house. That's our bedroom!'

Me: 'Where's ours?'

Dad: 'Um … Ah yes, lower ground floor, four further bedrooms, two with …'

Dontie: 'Lower ground floor? Does that mean they're underground? Awesome!'

Me: (worried) 'You need to go *up*stairs to bed.'

Mum: 'You don't *have* to.'

Stanley: (not sure) 'But you don't go *under*ground.'

Anika: (because Stanley's not sure) 'Don't like it.'

Mum: (cross) 'See what you've started now, Mattie?'

Me: (getting more and more worried,

on the verge of wailing) 'But I don't want to sleep underground!'

Dontie: '*I* do!'

Mum: (sighing) 'Stop arguing you lot. We'll find one that we all like.'

That's fine. But *we* don't get to see any more houses because Mum and Dad and the littlies go house-hunting when we're at school.

After a while I forget all about it. But then, one day Mum and Dad say they've seen a house they really, really, really like.

'That's not fair!' says V. 'You said we could help choose.'

'Yeah,' says Dontie. 'Dead right! If I've got to live in it, I've got to like it.'

'Well, come and see this one and see what you think,' says Mum. 'Then we can all decide together if we want to live in it.'

'What if I don't?' says Dontie who's set his heart on an underground bedroom.

'We'll leave you here,' says Dad.

He's just joking.

(I think.)

Chapter 14

On Saturday we all pile into our new car. It's big enough for all of us! We're going for a ride to see the new house. It's exciting!

'Jellico and Hiccup don't need to come with us,' says Dad when he spots them in the back.

'Yes they do,' I explain. 'It's going to be their new home too.'

Dad looks at Mum for help. Mum shrugs.

'Fair point,' says Dad.

It's quite a long way, so Mum's packed sandwiches for us. She lets me eat one on the way, and then V complains that the car smells of egg.

V gets grumpy in cars. Sometimes she gets sick too.

'Open the window!' orders Dad, so we do. But V is still cranky. She complains that Stanley is looking at her. Stan says, 'I'm not!' and V says, 'Yes you are!' so Mum tells him to look out of the window instead.

Then she complains that I'm breathing on her, and I say, 'I'm not!' and she says, 'Yes you are!' so I try not to breathe, but it's hard.

Then Will poos his nappy and everybody tries not to breathe.

It's not exciting anymore. I want to go home.

At last we come to a stop outside some big iron gates in the middle of nowhere. An estate agent in a smart suit is waiting for us with a clipboard. We follow his car up a long winding drive and when we go round the last bend the house is there in front of us.

'OMG!'

This is what I say when I see it for the first time. It's what Lucinda says when she's surprised. Normally I say *golly* or *gosh* but this house is definitely *OMG!*

Dontie says, 'It's awesome!'

V says, 'It's beautiful.'

Stanley says, 'It's flabbergasting.' He always thinks of the best words.

Anika and baby Will are speechless.

It's big and white, with a balcony and pillars each side of the front door. In front of the house is a lovely garden with clipped trees and flower beds and a big, sweeping lawn.

Jellico bounds around it, wagging his tail and barking his head off. Hiccup spots a flowerbed and hops over to nibble at it.

'I think they like it.'

Mum smiles at me. 'Granddad could play bowls on that grass,' she says.

'We could play tennis on it,' says Dontie. 'Like Wimbledon.'

'No need to, there's a court round the back,' says Dad, and he's not joking.

There's a swimming pool as well.

It feels like a dream.

'I thought you'd like it,' says Mum and her face is all shiny and smiley. She looks like Anika when she got her doll and pram for Christmas. 'Shall we have a look inside?'

It's just as beautiful indoors. The estate agent says we're allowed to explore, so we race around the house, calling out to each other.

'The rooms are MASSIVE!' yells Dontie.

'Well, we'll just have to shout to each other,' says Mum. 'We're good at that.'

'There are billions of bathrooms and shower-rooms,' reports V.

'Then we'll all be nice and clean,' says Mum.

'Except for Will,' says Dontie, and he chucks our baby brother under the chin. 'You'll still be stinky, won't you?' Will grins and kicks his legs in agreement.

'It's very neat and tidy,' I say.

'Don't worry, Mattie. It won't stay like that for long,' says Dad.

'Come and see!' shouts V from the landing. 'The living-room is upstairs.'

'That's so you get the best view,' explains Mum. 'Isn't it fantastic?'

We can see for miles.

'I can see the sea!' shouts V.

'Not quite,' says Mum.

'It's an upside-down house!' says V. 'Lily Pickles would like it.'

Lily Pickles is V's best friend, and she's always hanging upside-down off the bars at school.

'I'm going to count the bedrooms,' says V and tears off again.

I think about what V said and start to worry.

'You're quiet, Mattie,' says Mum, who doesn't miss a trick. 'What's up? Don't you like it?'

'If it's an upside-down house,' I say, 'where *are* the bedrooms?'

'Some are upstairs and some are downstairs.' Mum's face breaks into a smile. 'But none of them are underground. OK?'

I smile back, happy again. 'OK.'

V appears. 'There are seven bedrooms,' she announces importantly.

'Enough for one each,' says Dad. But he's wrong. I know all about rooms per person. I've done it in numeracy.

'No, there's not enough. There are eight of us now. Two people will have to share.'

'Not me!' says Dontie.

'Nor me!' says V.

'Stanley could share with Will,' I suggest, but Stanley looks alarmed.

'No!' he says. 'Will's too smelly!'

He's got a point.

'Oh dear,' says Dad, winking at Mum. 'We've got a bit of problem here. Seven bedrooms and eight people. What can we do?'

Nobody says anything. Dontie, V, Stanley and I want a bedroom to ourselves.

'What a shame,' says Mum. 'I really liked this house.'

'So did I,' says Dontie gloomily.

'Me too,' says V crossly.

'And me,' says Stan glumly.

'And me,' I say sadly.

'Tell you what,' Mum turns to Dad. 'I don't mind sharing. If you don't.'

'I don't mind sharing at all,' Dad says, and he and Mum smile their special smile at each other.

My mum and dad are really kind. Mum's been fed up with a tight squeeze for ages, and obviously she would prefer a bedroom to herself. I'm sure my dad would too.

Anyone would. It stands to reason.

Chapter 15

First thing Monday morning when we are doing silent reading, Lucinda says, 'Are you moving house?'

I stare at her in amazement.

'How do you know?'

Lucinda knows everything.

'My mum said. She says your mum and dad have been going round looking at houses.'

Actually, I think it's Lucinda's mum who knows everything, and she tells

Lucinda. Mum says if Lucinda's Mum doesn't know about something , it hasn't happened yet.

'Have you found one?'

'Yes.'

'What's it like?'

'Big and white.'

'Like mine?'

'Bigger.'

'Like Buckingham Palace?'

'Smaller. But it's got pillars and a balcony. And a swimming pool. And a tennis court.'

'It sounds like Buckingham Palace,' says Lucinda. 'Can you stand on the balcony and wave to people like the Queen?'

'No. There's no one to wave to. But you can see the sea.'

'Really?'

'Well, you could if it was a bit closer.'

'Lucinda and Mattie, stop talking,' shouts Miss Shoutalot.

'Sorry, Miss!'

'Can I come and swim in your pool?' continues Lucinda after a little while.

'Yes, if you want to,' I say.

'Can I come tomorrow after school?'

'I don't think we'll have moved in by then.'

'Can I come on Saturday after jazz and street dance?'

'If you like. I'll ask my mum.'

'Lucinda and Mattie, what did I say?' bawls Miss Shoutalot.

'Sorry, Miss!' Lucinda lowers her voice and says to me, 'My mum said to make sure I asked you how many bedrooms you've got in your new house.'

'Seven.'

'Can I sleep over on Saturday?'

'I'll ask my m...'

'Lucinda Packham-Wells and Mattie Butterfield, I'm not telling you again! KEEP QUIET!' bellows Miss Shoutalot, like an angry bull.

So we do.

At the end of school Mum is waiting for us as usual with Anika, Jellico and baby Will in his brand-new pram. She's surrounded by mums.

'Lovely new pram,' says one.

'For a lovely new baby,' coos another.

'Well, the old one was getting a bit tatty,' says Mum. I think she means the pram, not the baby.

'And I hear someone's got a new car

too,' remarks a third mum. I think she means us.

Is it my imagination, or do all these mums suddenly have green eyes?

Mum ignores her. 'Oh good, here they are,' she says, spotting us. She doesn't normally look *that* pleased to see us.

Lucinda tugs on her mum's arm but *her* mum is busy looking at *my* mum.

'Loving the new mac!' she says.

Mum's cheeks turn a bit pink. 'Time for a change,' she says.

'And the new bag!'

Mum's cheeks turn from pink to red. I don't think she really wants to speak to Lucinda's mum, or anyone else's mum for that matter, about our new things.

Lucinda tugs her mum's arm again but she shakes her off. 'You'll be moving

house next,' says Mrs Packham-Wells, her nose twitching with curiosity.

'Maybe,' says Mum. 'Time to go, kids.'

'Mum?' says Lucinda but she ignores her.

'Somewhere bigger?' Lucinda's mum persists.

'Mum! Listen! I'm trying to tell you …'

'Don't interrupt Lucinda. So, have you seen anything nice, Mona? What is it you're looking for? Four bedrooms? Can you stretch to five? The price shoots up of course once you pass three …'

'Seven,' says Lucinda.

Her mum and my mum both stare at Lucinda. So do all the other mums with wide green eyes.

'Seven,' repeats Lucinda. 'Their new house has got seven bedrooms. More than ours. That's what I've been trying to tell you.'

Lucinda's mum gives an embarrassed little giggle. 'You never know what she's going to come out with next.'

'But you asked me to find out.' Lucinda looks puzzled.

'No, I didn't,' says her mum faintly.

'Yes you did. Have you forgotten? This morning when you dropped me off. You said, now don't forget to ask Mattie if they've found a new house yet. Find out how many bedrooms it's got, you said. Remember?'

Mum raises her eyebrows. All the mums laugh as if Lucinda's said something funny. Except Mrs Packham-Wells. This time it's her turn to go bright red.

It's not a good look. It clashes with her green eyes.

Chapter 16

When Dad comes to tuck us into bed, I'm up on my knees staring out of the window. It's a full moon. Our back garden is full of sculptures that Dad makes us for our birthdays. They look magical tonight in the moonlight.

'Dad? Can we take our sculptures with us when we move house?'

'Um ... probably not.'

'Why not?' V sits bolt upright.

'Because they won't travel well. They'll

break into bits. Anyway, they won't like it in that new tidy garden. They want an old, overgrown wilderness to live in, like this one.'

'I'm not going anywhere without my birthday frog!' she squeals in panic.

'I'm not leaving Will the seal!' I squawk in alarm.

'OK, OK. Don't get your knickers in a twist. You can choose one each; we'll wrap them up carefully in newspaper and take them with us. But you'll have to leave the rest behind.'

'But what about the dragon?' whines V.

'And the dinosaurs?' groans me.

'And the dolphins?' wails V.

'And the hedgehog?' moans me.

'Kan-ga-rooooooooos?' whimpers a

small voice. Anika's woken up and now she's joining in, just as determined as we are.

'We'll see,' sighs Dad, which isn't good enough. When a grown-up says *we'll see* it really means *let's hope you've forgotten about it by the morning*.

But we won't.

After he's gone, I lie on my back listening to all the night-time sounds.

Outside my bedroom window, an owl is hooting in the tree.

A train chuffs past the bottom of our garden on its way to the sidings for the night.

Downstairs, Dad is whistling while he's washing up and the Corrie theme tune is warbling away on the telly. Mum's stretched out on the sofa, watching her favourite soap and feeding Will at the same time. She used to do that with Anika.

Nice sounds. Familiar sounds. Time-to-go-to-sleep-sounds.

I feel safe up here with my sisters snoring beside me. Turning over, I curl myself into V's nice warm back like I do every night and close my eyes, ready to fall fast asleep.

But I can't. My brain's gone into overdrive, and a nasty little voice is taunting me.

You won't be able to curl up next to V in the new house. She'll be in another room. So will Anika. You'll be on your own.

So? It's what I've always wanted – a bedroom to myself.

Isn't it?

Outside something is snuffling round the garden. What is it?

A badger? A cat?

A monster!

Get a grip, Mattie Worryguts. It doesn't matter what it is, you're safe up here.

You won't be safe in the new house though. You'll be sleeping on the ground floor. In the middle of nowhere. You can't see another house for miles.

Anything could knock on your window.

Anything could climb through your window!

A robber could get in! AND NOBODY WOULD KNOW!

I whimper. I don't like it. I don't want to be in a bedroom on my own after all. Those bedrooms in the new house are huge! I want to be snuggled up tight next to V. She'd tell the robber to go away. A robber would be scared of V.

I want to sleep upstairs.

I want to sleep with V.

I want to take *all* the sculptures with me to the new house.

Argh! I need to make a Worry List. But Mum will go mad if I wake up the others.

Go to sleep, Mattie. Stop worrying! Things will be better in the morning, they always are.

At last, with my arm round V's tummy, clinging onto her for dear life, I finally drop off to sleep.

But the next day, everything gets worse.

Chapter 17

Grandma and Granddad want to see the new house, so Dad drives them out there whilst we're at school. By the time we get home they're all sitting in the kitchen having a cup of tea.

'What did you think then?' asks Mum.

'Very nice,' says Grandma.

'Very nice indeed,' says Granddad.

But they don't sound very excited.

Usually when Grandma likes something, she goes on and on and on about it. But not today. Instead, she's quiet and thoughtful like she's got something on her mind.

'Did you like the kitchen?' asks Mum.

'Lovely.'

'What about the swimming pool?' says Dontie.

'Wonderful.'

'The garden's HUGE!' says Stanley.

'H-U-G-E!' repeats Anika, stretching her arms wide. Actually, it's a lot bigger than that.

'That'll keep you busy, Tim,' says Granddad.

'Don't fancy a job do you?' says Dad.

Granddad snorts. 'Long way to go to cut the grass.'

'It'll be funny not being able to pop in whenever we feel like it,' says Grandma, sounding sad. 'Don't suppose we'll be seeing so much of you all from now on.'

I stare at her in surprise. I never thought of that. Grandma and Granddad pop in most days, usually at tea-time. Sometimes it gets on Mum's nerves when they come because it's the busiest time of day what with tea and homework and getting the littlies to bed. But they've always done it, it's part of our lives.

Now I feel sad at the thought of not seeing them so much. I think Anika does too because she goes and lays her head in Grandma's lap. Grandma strokes her hair and looks like she's going to cry.

And the funny thing is, Mum looks like she's going to cry too. A minute later, Uncle Vez pops his head round the door.

'How do?'

We see Uncle Vez nearly every day too. He does odd jobs for us like digging the garden, and Mum makes sure he has his tea with us before he goes home because she worries that he doesn't bother to cook. Uncle Vez is part of the family.

He says we keep him young, but he's even older than Grandma and Granddad. Today he looks like a pirate with a parrot on his shoulder. Although it's a rabbit rather than a parrot. Hiccup is my rabbit, but I think he loves Uncle Vez best. I don't mind. We all love Uncle Vez.

When he sits down, Hiccup jumps onto the back of the chair. Uncle Vez fishes his biro out of his jacket pocket and takes a few puffs. He smokes a biro instead of a cigarette since Aunty Etna died. Aunty Etna and Uncle Vez were Mum's foster parents when she was growing up.

He's all alone now. Except for us.

'Quiet in here,' remarks Uncle Vez, but no one answers.

'Cat got your tongues?' he asks. He's only joking. We haven't got a cat.

'Come on then,' he says after a while. 'What's up? Spill the beans.'

'We've found a new house,' says Dad.

'Oh aye? What's it like?'

'Very nice,' says Grandma.

'Very nice indeed,' says Granddad.

'Well that's good news,' says Uncle Vez. 'Isn't it?'

'It's a long way away,' I explain.

'Aahh,' he says. 'How long?'

'Just an hour or two in the car,' says Dad, which makes it sound not too far away. Then I remember that Uncle Vez can't drive.

'Can't you find something a bit closer?' he asks.

'No,' says Mum. 'We've looked everywhere.'

'Right.' Uncle Vez puts his biro back in his mouth and reaches for Hiccup. He sits there stroking the rabbit silently with his kind hands. Hiccup practically purrs with pleasure.

Actually, Uncle Vez looks more like a garden gnome than a pirate. An old one, a bit chipped and broken. His hands and face are covered in brown sunspots. That's because he's always in the garden.

Last spring he planted a vegetable patch for us. Grandma helped him. We sold vegetables out the front and made £8.31 for the new baby.

Mum keeps an eye on him now. It's only fair because he kept an eye on her when she was young.

I don't want to leave Uncle Vez on his own. I don't want to leave Grandma and Granddad on their own either.

I've got a lump in my throat and my eyes are prickly.

I don't want to go and live in the new house any more.

Chapter 18

At playtime I'm sitting with my back against the wall, watching Lucinda leaping around in front of me. She's tossing her hair, wobbling her legs, pointing her elbows out at right angles and waving her arms. This is because she's showing me what she learned in Dance Class on Saturday.

Lucinda is my best friend.

Across the playground I can see my brother Stanley doing a backwards running race with Rupert Rumble. Stanley is getting better at it, but he still loses every time. This is because Rupert Rumble is amazing at doing things backwards. He can count backwards and say the alphabet backwards and write backwards, and now he's teaching Stanley how to do it too.

Rupert Rumble is Stanley's best friend.

Over by the bins, I can see my sister V and Lily Pickles hanging upside-down off the bars having a chat. They do this all the time. Lily Pickles' hair hangs down to the ground and V's bunches stick out at the side. Mrs Beasely on playground duty used to tell them off, but now she doesn't even notice. V says Lily Pickles says you can think better upside down because all the blood rushes to your head.

Lily Pickles is V's best friend.

It's nice having a best friend. You can learn a lot from them. Today I'm learning jazz and street dance from Lucinda who chants things like 'Step-step, basic turn,' as she throws herself around. I have to concentrate very hard, and it stops me from thinking about moving house.

'Can I have a go now?' I ask, and at last Lucinda says yes. I scramble to my feet and stand next to her awaiting instructions.

'Copy me,' she says and flings her right arm out stiffly in front of her, then bends her head and lifts her left knee at the same time. I do exactly the same.

'Not like that,' she says. 'Watch.' So I do.

V appears in front of me with Lily

Pickles. Something is wrong.

My sister V is often cross, frequently funny, always brave, usually impatient, generally kind, sometimes naughty and occasionally sorry. But, unlike me, she never, ever, *ever* worries about anything.

Even when she couldn't read because she couldn't see the letters on the page, she just pretended she could but didn't want to. She got into loads of trouble at school. (This is actually not a good thing to do. Luckily Grandma sorted it all out, but that's another story).

I'm the worrier in the family, not V.

But today she is looking **VERY WORRIED INDEED!**

Stanley and Rupert Rumble come over to find out what is going on.

'What's wrong, V?'

A tear rolls down her cheek. 'I DON'T WANT TO MOVE SCHOOLS!' she bawls. Lily Pickles bursts into tears too.

'Why do you have to move schools?' asks Lucinda, puzzled.

'Because (*sob*) … the new house (*hiccup*)… is a long way away (*splutter*) … and Lily says (*croak*) … I won't be

able to come to this school (*sob*) … an-y-mooooore.' (*Wail!*)

I stare at my distraught little sister who hated school not so long ago, and my little brother who's loved school from day one. Stanley looks stunned.

OH NO!

We're going to have to move schools.

Why didn't I think of that?

Chapter 19

In the afternoon we do creative writing. We are allowed to write about anything we want so long as it's in silence. Mrs Shoutalot has got a headache.

I've got a headache too. My brain is all tangled up like spaghetti.

Mum says that when my brain gets tangled up I should make a Worry List and then my worries will go away. So I do.

This is what I write.

WORRY LIST

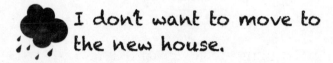 I don't want to move to the new house.

I don't want to move away from Uncle Vesuvius.

I don't want to move away from Grandma and Granddad.

I don't want to move away from Lucinda.

I don't want to move schools.

I don't want to move. Full stop.

'Is that a poem?' asks Lucinda.

'No, it's a Worry List.'

'Let's see.' She reads it through. And then, BIG SURPRISE! Two fat tears spill out of Lucinda's eyes and trickle down her cheeks.

I have never, in my whole life, seen Lucinda cry. Not even when her mum and dad didn't like each other very much.

When I come out of school, Mum knows straight away something is wrong.

'Uh oh! You've got your Worry Face on,' she sighs.

Stan appears beside us looking glum. Normally he charges around the playground playing fighter planes with Rupert Rumble but today he just stands still, staring at his feet.

Mum looks at him suspiciously. 'What's wrong with you?' she asks.

Before he can answer, V bursts out of her classroom door like a jack-in-the-box, yelling, 'IT'S NOT FAIR!'

Mum holds up her hand. 'Hold it right there!' she commands, looking round at the other mums who have stopped talking to listen. 'We'll talk about this on the way home.'

When we've left the mums far behind, she says, 'Right then. Spit it out.'

'I'm not going!' says V.

'Going where?' says Mum.

'To the new house.'

Mum rolls her eyes. 'What a surprise.'

'I'm not going either,' says Stanley bravely, and Mum looks startled.

'Nor me,' I say, and now Mum looks really alarmed.

So am I. I didn't know I was going to

say that until it came out of my mouth. But the funny thing is, I mean it.

'What's brought all this on?' she asks.

'We can't move house,' I explain, 'because if we do, we'll have to move schools.'

'Ah!' She looks as guilty as Jellico when he's been caught licking plates.

My heart sinks. It's true then.

'We were going to talk to you about that.'

'When?'

'When the time was right. I know what you're like, Worry-Guts.'

'I don't want to move schools!' I moan.

'Now, don't start, Mattie! There's

nothing to worry about. It's a really nice school, you'll love it there.'

'*I* won't,' says V.

This is probably true. V took ages to settle into school. But Mum's not ready to give up yet.

'Don't be silly. You'll all make lots of new friends, how nice will that be? They'll be queuing up around the block to be friends with you.'

This is probably not true. There might be a little queue for Stanley and there may be one or two for me, but unless the new school has its own Lily Pickles, it's unlikely anyone will be queuing up to be friends with V (no offence, V).

I sigh heavily. She just doesn't get it.

Me: 'That's not the point.'

Mum: (getting cross) 'What *is* the point

then, Mattie?'

Me: 'Lucinda can't manage without me.'

V: 'And Lily can't manage without me.'

Stan: 'And Rupert Rumble can't manage without me.'

Mum's eyes go soft and swimmy.

Me: (in case, she still hasn't got it) 'And Uncle Vesuvius can't manage without you.'

Mum's eyes go shiny and wet.

V: 'And Grandma and Granddad can't manage without any of us.'

Mum: (eyes spilling over, just like Lucinda's) 'I don't know! I wish we'd never won the flipping lottery!'

Oh no! Now we're for it! It's all my fault, I started it. V, Stanley, Anika, Will and I, stare at her, round-eyed, as she scrubs the tears away, blows her nose and takes a deep breath.

'Right, that's it!' she says. 'I've made my mind up.'

Sticking her chin out just like V's, she takes off with the pram so fast that we have to chase after her to keep up.

Chapter 20

As soon as we get home from school, Mum yells 'TIM!'

Dad comes running in from the shed.

'What's wrong?'

'Ring your mum and dad and tell them to get round here quick. Mattie? Run round the corner and fetch Uncle Vesuvius.'

'What shall I say?'

'Tell him to come straight away.'

Oh flip! I'm in serious trouble. Mum's

mad at me because I don't want to move to the new house anymore. She's going to tell everyone what a bad, ungrateful girl I am.

This is the worst day of my life. It's all my Worry Lists come true.

When I get back with Uncle Vez, a man is getting out of a van with a 'FOR SALE' sign. It makes me feel funny to think that soon another family will be living in our house.

Grandma and Granddad pull up in their car.

'Where's the fire?' asks Granddad.

'Mum's on the warpath!' I say miserably. 'I'm in big trouble.'

'Oh dear,' says Granddad, putting an arm round my shoulders. 'Let's go in and face the music, shall we?'

Inside, Mum and Dad are standing on the rug in front of the fire. They look very serious. Dad is holding a shoebox.

Dontie is home and sitting up to attention. So are the others (but not Will, he can't sit up yet. He's asleep in his pram).

It feels like school when Mrs Shoutalot is cross with us. Granddad, Grandma and Uncle Vesuvius must think so too because they pluck V, Stanley and Anika into their laps and sit down without a word.

To my surprise Dad opens the shoebox and hands us each a piece of paper and a pencil.

'What's all this about?' asks Granddad.

'I gather,' says Mum sternly, 'that some people in this family don't want us to move to our new dream house.'

'Well, nobody's actually said that ...' says Grandma nervously.

'Oh yes they have,' says Mum, staring at me, and I wish I was invisible. 'So we're going to settle this once and for all.'

'We're putting it to the vote,' explains Dad. 'If you want us to move, put a tick.'

'And if you don't, put a cross,' adds Mum.

'There's only one condition. You must tell the truth, each and every one of you,' instructs Dad. 'Including you.' He fixes Grandma, Granddad and Uncle Vez with a beady eye and they nod.

'Mum gets Will's vote,' says Dad and V opens her mouth to object then closes it again. I know what she's thinking – *it's not fair!* But it is. Will has to go wherever

Mum goes so it's up to her.

'And Mattie,' adds Mum, kindly. 'There's no need to worry. You won't get into trouble, whatever you decide.'

'It's a secret ballot,' says Dad. 'So nobody will know who puts a tick or a cross. You put your voting slip in this box here.' He points to the shoebox and I notice it's got a hole cut in the top. 'Then we count them when we've all voted.'

'It's a free democratic election,' explains Dontie, who likes to show off now he's at big school. 'The majority vote wins, right?'

'That's right,' says Dad. 'Eleven people are voting. If six people or more put a tick, we'll be going. But if six people or more put a cross, then we're staying.'

I look around at my funny family.

Dad, Mum, Dontie and Will will be in the *I want to move* camp.

V, Stan and me will be in the *I want to stay* camp.

Anika? She'll do whatever Stan wants.

But – WORRY ALERT! – she won't know what he wants because it's a secret ballot! And it's much easier to make a tick than a cross when you're only three years old.

And what about Grandma, Granddad and Uncle Vez? They don't want us to move away. But grown-ups are funny, you can never tell what they're going to do.

MASSIVE HUMUNGOUS WORRY ALERT!

'Sounds fair?' asks Dad.

'Sounds fair to me,' says Granddad.

'And me,' says Uncle Vez.

'Right then, make your choice,' says Dad.

I draw a cross, fold it over and place it in the box.

Chapter 21

The vote is unanimous. That means we all voted the same. And the most amazing thing is, we all voted to stay!

I can't believe my eyes when every single piece of paper, one after the other, reveals a cross. It's the best moment of my life. Even Mum and Dad have voted to stay. And Dontie! I never expected that!

'Dontie? I thought you wanted to move to the new house?'

'I did, till Mum and Dad told me I'd have to move schools. I've only just started a new one. I don't want to move again.'

'When did they tell you that?' says V, cross that they'd told him and not the rest of us.

'Today, when I came home from school.'

So that was OK then. I beam at Mum. Then I remember that she was looking forward to living in her lovely new house.

'Mum? Are you sad?'

'No, Mattie, not a bit. I think your dad and I got carried away with it all. It was a nice house but it's too far away. We'll have to move at some point though because ...'

'... it's a tight squeeze!' We all finish

her sentence for her and she laughs.

'Yes it is. But we'll just have to wait till the right one comes up closer to home.'

Suddenly my hand flies to my mouth and I gasp in horror.

'What is it now, Mattie?' asks Mum wearily.

'It's too late!' I howl. 'We're going to have to move after all!'

'What's she going on about?' asks Dontie.

'The 'FOR SALE' sign! It's already gone up. The man brought it in his van.'

'Really?' Dad looks puzzled.

'There was a man with a sign outside,' agrees Uncle Vez.

We rush to the window and press our faces against the glass. I was right. There it is, by the front gate, under the lamplight.

'That's strange,' says Mum.

'I didn't know you'd already put it up for sale,' says Grandma.

'We haven't,' says Dad, peering through the window. 'Oh, I see …' he chuckles, '… it's on the other side of the fence. It's in next door's garden.'

'Soooo …' says Mum thoughtfully, '… that means next door is up for sale?'

'Looks like,' grins Dad. 'Interesting.'

'Well, well, well,' says Granddad.

'Be easy enough to knock through,' says Uncle Vez.

'Easy as pie,' says Dad.

'You'd have a house double the size of this one, then,' says Grandma.

'Double!' repeats Mum. 'Fancy that!'

'So we'd still get to live here?' asks V.

'Here and next door. We could make it

into one house big enough for all of us,' says Dad.

'All of us? Grandma and Granddad too?' asks Stanley.

'No, no,' says Grandma quickly. 'We've got our own house.'

'What about Uncle Vez?' I ask.

Mum and Dad look at each other and smile.

'What about it, Uncle Vez?' repeats Mum. 'Do you think you could put up with us all?'

Uncle Vez takes his biro out of his pocket and gives it a puff while he considers.

'I reckon I could give it a go,' he says finally, and we all cheer.

'And we definitely, definitely, definitely, wouldn't have to move schools?' I ask, just to make sure.

'No, of course not.'

'And I'd get a bedroom of my own?' Dontie asks.

'Yep.'

'And a computer in my room?'

'Don't push it, sunshine,' says Dad, and they grin at each other.

'Can we buy it then?' pleads V.

'Can we?'

'Please?'

'It's up to your mum.'

Mum hesitates. Then her face breaks into a big, beautiful smile.

'It's a yes from me.'

We jump up and down, yelling and shouting, and wake baby Will up.

So he joins in too.

Chapter 22

I'm in bed, warm as toast, curled up tight round V. Hiccup is fast asleep like a furry, quivery hot-water bottle by my feet. He's been allowed in tonight because it's so cold outside. Beside me Anika is snoring tunefully.

The train rattles past the end of the garden on its way home to the sidings.

Going-to-sleep

Going-to-sleep

Going-to-sleep

Dad's piled heavy coats on top of our

duvets to keep us cosy. The man on the telly said it might snow tomorrow!

But though I'm tired, I'm too excited to sleep.

We're-stay-ing-at-home
We're-buy-ing-next-door
We're-not-going-to-move

We won't have to move schools. And we won't be crowded anymore!

I'm so happy I give V a big squeeze. She wriggles away from me, grumbling in her sleep, so I let go and hug myself instead.

It's strangely light outside. Like aliens have landed.

I hope my seal is OK in the garden. I'd better check on him.

Fighting my way through coats and duvets, I crawl to the bottom of the bed and pull back the curtain.

I don't believe it! It's snowing already!

Flakes are floating down from the sky and landing on the statues. Some of them are already hidden from sight, but I can still make out snow-sharks and snow-dragons and a snow-seal called Will.

I watch the snowflakes floating and dancing, whirling and swirling, casting a spell on our garden, transforming it from a wilderness to a magical world of white.

I love my garden.

I love my home.

I love my funny family.